ORION CHILDREN'S BOOKS

First published in Great Britain in 2014 by Orion Children's Books
This edition published in 2018 by Hodder and Stoughton

3 5 7 9 10 8 6 4 2 1

A CIP catalogue record for this book
is available from the British Library.

ISBN 978 1 51010 558 4

Printed and bound in China
The paper and board used in this book are from
well-managed forests and other responsible sources.

MIX
Paper from
responsible sources
FSC® C104740
FSC
www.fsc.org

Orion Children's Books
An imprint of
Hachette Children's Group
Part of Hodder and Stoughton
Carmelite House
50 Victoria Embankment
London EC4Y 0DZ

An Hachette UK Company
www.hachette.co.uk
www.hachettechildrens.co.uk

*For my dad, who found
the first shell* – M.S.

*For lovely little
Eliza* – A.W.

Milly AND the MERMAIDS

MAUDIE SMITH ANTONIA WOODWARD

Orion
Children's Books

Milly was on her way to the seaside. "Do you think we'll see a mermaid?" she asked.

Dad laughed. "You never know!" he said.

Milly built a sandcastle. She decorated it with seaweed and made a wide moat for mermaids to swim in.

"Any mermaids yet?" said Mum.
"Not yet," said Milly. "But
you never know!"

Milly buried Mum up to her waist.
She gave her sandy scales and a long
mermaid tail.

The real mermaids would be sure to
want to come and see the Mum Mermaid.
Mermaids were very curious.

But Mum didn't stay as a mermaid for long.
She stood up to find the sandwiches and left
her tail behind.

sniff
sniff

"Any mermaids yet?" asked Dad.

"Not yet," said Milly. "But you never know!"

Milly drew a lovely big face in the sand.

"Is that you?" said Dad.

"Of course it's not me," said Milly. "It's a mermaid."

Milly thought the mermaids might see the face and come to take a closer look.

But the mermaids didn't come. A dog came and he dug a hole. He sent sand scattering all over the place.

"My mermaid!" cried Milly.

Milly sat on a rock and wished for mermaids.
She wished and wished but no mermaids came.
Only the sea swept in and whispered,

"You never know! You never know!"

Dad was coming along the beach. Milly could see
something in his hand. It was shimmery blue and glittery
green. It looked exactly like a tiny mermaid!

It wasn't though. It was only a seashell.

"I don't want a stupid seashell!" said Milly.

"I want **a mermaid!**"

And she threw the shell in the sand.

But when it was time to go, they
took the seashell home.

That night, by Milly's bed, the seashell started to grow.

It grew and it grew

until it filled the room.

Milly went inside and found...

...a mermaid!

The mermaid tossed her shimmery blue
hair and smiled. She held out her glittery
green hand.

Milly swam with the mermaids…

Milly played with the mermaids…

...all the way till morning.

Then Milly and the mermaids
said goodbye.

"I love my seashell, Dad," said Milly.

"That's good," said Dad. "I'm sorry we didn't see a mermaid though."

"I'd love to see a mermaid," said Mum. "Do you think we ever will?"

Milly smiled. "You never know!" she said. "You never know!"